What the Mouse Found
and Other Stories

and Other Stories

What the Mouse Found

and Other Stories

Charles de Lint

SUBTERRANEAN PRESS • 2008

First Edition

ISBN: 978-1-59606-159-0

Subterranean Press
PO Box 190106
Burton, MI 48519

www.subterraneanpress.com

still for
Adam & Kmoré,
Christine, Mary & Sophie

Table of Contents

INTRODUCTION:

Kissing Frogs

KISSING FROGS.

It's one of the classic images from fairy tales. And in its few short pages, the story itself touches on any number of universal themes: faith, humility, loyalty, kindness—the sorts of things that well-meaning adults don't appear to see when they forbid their children from reading fairy tales because they're too scary, or violent, or might instill in them the virus of witchcraft (which we all know leads straight to drugs, Goth culture, and who knows what other terrible evils).

It's all nonsense, of course.

Fairy tales prepare the reader for the world as it is, not how we'd like it to be, and offer some guideposts to take us through the worst of the real world's dark forests and lonely stretches of desolate lands. I understand a parent's desire to protect their children from the evils of the world. The problem is, to send them out with no concept of the dangers, carries its own risks.

Fairy tales also do a wonderful job of instilling a moral compass in the reader. They certainly do a better job than following the exploits of sports figures, actors, rock stars, and those individuals who are famous just for being famous.

But neither of those benefits is the best reason to read them. That would be for their quirky wonder and how they allow us to imagine the world to be a bigger and even more interesting place than we think it is.

They can also awake a love for books that might stay with a child through their teenage years and into adulthood.

At least it did for me.

Now I had none of this in mind when I was writing the stories collected here. They were written for nieces, nephews and the children of friends—most of the stories accompanying dolls and toys that MaryAnn had made for them. In fact, the best part of putting this collection together was digging out photos of those dolls. It wasn't until I found the photos that the stories came alive for me again, reminding me of the child the story was written for. Because they're all grown up now. Some have changed their names (hello, Mary!) or have moved away and are no longer a part of our lives. None of them are who they were at the time.

But I treasure the memories these photos and stories call up when I read them again.

They were all written in the eighties (copyright notices notwithstanding) when MaryAnn was making any number of toys and dolls, along with larger whimsical fabric maché sculptures. There was a point when our house was filled with her creations and it could be quite startling coming upon some of the life-sized ones—especially for visitors.

I remember we lived in a three story half-double back then. The third floor attic had been renovated and I kept my books and videos up there, along with a life-sized sculpture of a granny that gave one of my nieces a real scare when she went up to choose a movie one evening. That was when "granny" stood by the stairs. After

11

that, I moved her to the attic's single window so that she could look out at the street.

A few weeks later, a woman from across the street came over and mentioned that her two boys were a little freaked by the old lady who was always standing in the window, staring at them.

We also had any number of smaller sculptures on shelves and speakers and the tops of buffets: old men playing chess, an elfin harper, a lady with a wardrobe out of Wal-Mart playing bingo. There was a life-sized skateboarder, and we still have a jester sitting up on a bookshelf, as well as Diefenbaker the bull dog standing guard in whatever room we've got him guarding (it changes).

And then there were all those dolls and toys. Beanbag bears and rabbits. Funny little flying fairies and angels. Some had whole dioramas made for them that hung on the wall, like a teddy bear's picnic with dozens of little bears you could move around in the scene.

Lovely stuff. And they all had stories, I'm sure, though I only wrote about the ones you find collected here.

Some of these stories wear their influences stronger than others. If you can't find my love for Kenneth Grahame and A.A. Milne in a couple, you aren't looking hard enough. But by the time I got to "Tip & the Lion" I was already starting to find a voice for my short fiction, and it seems better for it—at least it does to me.

That said, the two stories set in the Eastern woodlands of Quebec ("Oakey Bedokey" and "Maple Sugar") have a different kind of charm for me since they call up the memories of my nephew Adam and (cover girl!) niece Kmoré in the way back when. MaryAnn and I have an old schoolbus on the lake near the cabin where they lived when they were young and it was an easy trek through the woods to visit. We even cut a path through the woods and built a little bridge over the stream to make it easier to get back and forth from their log cabin home up on the hill to our old bus.

The kids are grown now, ready to start families of their own. The bridge is washed away and the path is overgrown. But we still trek (by the road, these days) up to their parents' cabin and take part in many a meal and share their good company.

And the stories are still here, shared now with a wider audience.

I hope you enjoy them. And please, read them to your favourite small one. And don't forget to show them the pictures. You can tell them that Oakey Bedokey and Maple Sugar still live in that log cabin in the woods. Because they do.

Do the toys come alive when people aren't looking? I don't know. I also don't know that it matters.

It's like kissing frogs. Mostly, they're just frogs— but after all, isn't a frog a marvel, all on its own?

—Charles de Lint
Ottawa,
winter 2008

What the Mouse Found

IT WAS A NIGHT of moonlight and silver, when the grass stalks whispered quietly to each other in the Big Field and clouds like tall ships sailed across the sky. Christopher Mouse was walking down the Faraway Path that leads a twisty way from the Badger's Oak in the middle of the Branching Wood, all the way to the Wide World beyond. He wore a small red cap on his head and a green scarf, and smoked an acorn pipe that trailed smoke behind him like a cloak of ribbons caught in the wind.

It was a night for watching and listening, and Christopher was doing just that. He stopped to look at a perfectly round pebble, and again at a curiously shaped bit of wood that looked just like a button, complete with two tiny holes for the thread. He listened to what the grasses said to each other and to the windy call of the cloud ships as they crossed the sky. He even listened to the scuff of his own small feet on the path—when he wasn't stopped, just looking and smelling and hearing the world turn around him.

It was a night of mystery and a time for finding things, when secrets slipped out from under stones and danced in the moonlight, and when the stars crept down, one by one, to bathe in the deep pool near the Badger's Oak before returning to the dark skies in a rush of smiles and teasing starish laughter. A special night, Christopher knew, and coming around the bulk of a tall stone, he knew why.

Lying there on the path was a small limp figure, and standing over it was Jack Nab Raven, his black feathers all a-rustle and the string of Gypsy beads he wore about his neck click-clacking against each other as his head moved from side to side, sharp dark eyes fixed on that small still form.

"Well," Christopher said.

And then: "Oh, my."

And finally: "Hello, Jack Nab. What are you up to tonight?"

"Found something, I have, Mister Mouse, sir. Have indeed."

"Indeed you have," Christopher murmured.

What it was was a bean-bag rabbit with floppy ears and floppy limbs and a little round bunch of a tail. Christopher poked at a leg with his small paw. The rabbit seemed to be made of felt. A toy rabbit. And it was as big as Christopher Mouse—which, while it made Jack Nab's find seem huge to Christopher, in truth made it not very big at all. Christopher was, after all, a mouse. But he thought it was a most enormous toy.

It all had something to do with Perspective, Badger had explained to him one night, and Christopher had nodded sagely, not quite sure what the old fellow meant, but willing to go along with him as he obviously knew more on the subject than Christopher did himself.

"I never hurt it," Jack Nab was saying somewhat worriedly. "I just found it, I did, sir. Lying still. Just like that."

"Hmmm," Christopher said.

"What do you suppose it is?" Jack Nab asked.

"Well now," Christopher said. "I don't know. It looks like a toy, but it's much too big to be one. We could ask Badger, but this looks like it was made by Big Folk, and while Badger knows all there is to know about woodish things and fieldish things and other things besides, he doesn't know as much about Big Folkish things."

Jack Nab waited expectantly, happy that there was someone else to make a decision for him. He was a Gypsyish sort of bird, who liked to travel and collect odd bits of this and that, but not at all fond of puzzles. This was mostly because he wasn't very good at them.

"What shall we do?" he asked finally.

Christopher just smiled and then he said: "Would you give us a lift on those strong wings of yours?"

So Jack Nab Raven flew back into the Branching Wood, with Christopher perched on his neck, one arm holding tightly onto their find, the other wrapped about the raven's neck. They flew high above the Big Field, though not as high as the cloud ships, and landed in front of a tall elm tree that had a door in its side, and a window beside that, and a candle in the window that cast a pleasant glow on the windowsill and the ground in front of it. With a certain amount of awkwardness—limp bundles are never easy to manage—Christopher clambered down from Jack Nab's neck without losing the hold he had on the toy rabbit. Then he laid it on the ground, tapped with a small paw at the door, and waited.

There came an "I wonder who that could be" from inside, followed by a sound at the door, then the knob turned and a small dark-haired girl peered out at what the night had deposited on her doorstep.

Her name was Sophie and she lived in the Branching Wood—but only at night while she was sleeping at home in her house in a big city that was in the Wide World, far away from the forest, and sometimes in the afternoon when she was having a nap. Christopher knew her very well because she was always willing to share a cup of hot chocolate with him and had a great deal of interesting things to tell him that no one else could. She was not properly a Big Folk (but that was only because she was still a little girl), and privately he called her Wise Sophie, because that was how she seemed to him.

"Well," she said. "What brings you here tonight, Christopher Mouse and Jack Nab Raven?"

"Well, now," Christopher replied, "we've found something that needs explaining, Sophie…"

With that he stepped aside to show her what he and Jack Nab had found. Sophie smiled when she saw the floppy-eared rabbit.

"Why, it's Bunnypaws!" she said.

"I never tried to hurt it," Jack Nab explained, nervous once more. "I just found it, Miss Sophie, lying all still like that."

"Do you know what it is?" Christopher asked.

"Of course I do. He lives in my house back home." (By which she meant her other home in the Wide World where she lived when she wasn't sleeping and dreaming of being in the Branching Wood.)

"Is it dead?" Jack Nab asked.

Sophie laughed. "No, silly! It's a toy."

"So that's why it just sort of lies there," Christopher said, "even though it's too big to be a toy for someone my size?"

"That's exactly why!"

"Oh, well," Christopher said, as if to say, *he* knew *that*.

Sophie reached down to pick up the toy and then a curious thing happened. No sooner did her fingers touch the toy rabbit than it sat up, blinked its eyes and looked around at them—seeming almost as surprised as they were.

"Oh, dear," Sophie said.

"Oh, my," Christopher said.

"I never hurt it," Jack Nab said.

"Hello," Bunnypaws said.

The toy rabbit slapped its felt paws together and

regarded each of them in turn with a tilt to its head.

There was a long moment of silence. Sophie looked at the toy rabbit and it looked back at her. Christopher looked at them looking at each other, and thought to himself, well, indeed, it was that sort of night, wasn't it? The sort of night when anything could happen, and somewhere it probably did, only tonight it had happened here and to them. He saw that Jack Nab was still nervously ruffling his feathers and his beads were still clicking-clacking against each other while he muttered things like "I never" and "To think!" Sophie herself seemed a little astonished and not quite sure *what* to do, while Bunnypaws just sat there blinking and looking about himself with a happy look on his face.

Christopher glanced up and saw that the moon was still away up high, lighting the sails of the cloud ships, and the grasses were still murmuring to each other in the Big Field, though it was harder to hear them from here in the wood, because all the leaves were gossiping to each other and making bit of a row. And yes, he thought, it was that sort of a night and, feeling a bit wise himself just then, he knew that it wasn't a time for gaping and wondering and thinking about things, because it was altogether the wrong sort of a night for it.

"Do you have any hot chocolate?" he asked Sophie.

She stirred, looked at him, and then smiled.

"Why, yes," she said. "Yes, I do. Why don't we all go inside and have some."

And that's exactly what they did, Jack Nab and Christopher and Sophie and Bunnypaws (who was a little wobbly on his feet at first) and they made quite an evening out of it. And after that Bunnypaws lived with Sophie in her elm tree house and, while he was just a toy in the Wide World when Sophie was awake, there in the Branching Wood they lived happily ever after indeed. ✷

Gnomin' in The Gloamin'

THERE WAS A WEE bit of a man who lived under the neighbours' hedge and you couldn't see him even if you looked very hard, but he was there all the same. He was a gnome—not the sort with a tall red peaked cap and a Santa Claus beard like in the picture books, but he was just as small, maybe smaller, and if he wasn't a gnome, then what was?

That's what Opa Jan—Christine's granddad said.

The gnome wasn't alone either. There were all sorts of little folk who lived in hedges and trees, at the bottoms of gardens and even in Susan's playhouse, though she'd never seen one. They were very careful about being seen. They had to be. There were dogs to worry about, when they ran loose, and cats all the time. But at night, when the world lay still, they crept out. And sometimes they gathered food, like acorns or a bean from the garden in summer. And sometimes they were out to get twigs for their fires or the smallest of withies for their baskets. And sometimes they were out just because the moon was full and they wanted to dance in her light.

"Even in the winter?" Christine had asked. "When it's oh so cold?"

"Even in the winter," Opa Jan replied. "They go sleighing then, and sliding and skating."

"But what do they eat?"

"They store their food—like squirrels do."

Christine liked squirrels and she loved her granddad, but she wasn't sure if she believed in his gnomes. For one thing, he said there was nothing horrible living in the basement and Christine *knew* a horrible thing lived there. It was the cousin of whatever it was that breathed in her closet some nights and probably the brother of what lived under her bed when the lights went out, just waiting for her to let slip a hand or a foot over the edge of the bed. It was no good looking to see if they were there, for they were better at hiding than just about anybody. Christine supposed they'd had lots of practice.

Opa Jan said there was nothing to see because there was nothing there.

But he also said there were gnomes.

They couldn't both be true. So one night, in the middle of December when her parents went out to a party and her brother was in his bedroom listening to Twisted Sister records and talking on the phone, Christine got ready to go gnoming. She waited until Opa Jan had fallen asleep in front of the TV, then bundled up as warmly as she could and went to sit on the steps outside her house, very quietly. And there she waited.

There wasn't much snow yet—nothing at all on their lawn—but it was cold that night. Too cold for gnomes, probably, she thought after a few minutes, especially gnomes without red hats and white beards. But she waited some more. She watched her breath. Picking up a twig, she pretended it was a cigarette and her breath was the smoke, then decided that even pretending to smoke couldn't be very good for you. She'd hate to be coughing all the time like Opa Jan. So she threw away the twig and sat some more. And thought some more.

What if with every breath you let out you lost a bit of yourself? She remembered Opa Jan being a lot bigger than he was now. Was that what had happened to him? But then she thought of Susan's little brother.

If he lost a bit of himself every time he breathed, he'd soon be worn away to nothing. Except he just kept getting bigger. Maybe for the first half of your life your breathing added something, and then it started to take something away after—when you were older.

It certainly was cold.

Maybe she should get up and march up and down the walk like a soldier. Except then the noise she'd make would scare away the gnomes. If there even were gnomes. Which she doubted. But there was something in the basement. What if it came outside at night and was just waiting to find a little girl all by herself, sitting on the steps like she was? It would be a big something, too. She just knew it. A horrible something.

She shivered then and it wasn't from the cold. She looked back at the house. The living room looked funny from out here. It was lit by the TV and the light that came through the window was constantly moving and changing. If the thing from the basement came outside and grabbed her and she screamed, nobody would hear her. Not Opa Jan, asleep in front of the TV. Not her brother, who was listening to his horribly loud music. Not her parents, who weren't even home. Not anyone. This was what it was like to be the last person alive in the world. You had to sit on a porch in the cold and when you screamed, no one heard you. And there wouldn't be any gnomes either.

She was about to get up and go inside then when she heard a sound. Not a proper sound. More a sidling sort of trying-to-be-quiet sound. Christine's throat went all dry. She wanted to get up but she was too scared to move. So she just sat there, listening. She looked down the walk and onto the street, but there was nothing there. She looked along the porch, but there was nothing there either. Nothing anywhere. Except something had made a sound. Some *thing*. And she knew what it was. It lived in her basement and was always hungry for little girls and it was awful and it was outside in the night with her. Right now. She was just sure it was going to—

If she'd gone still before, now she went the stillest she'd ever been. She didn't even breathe. For there, crossing the lawn on cat-quiet feet, was a little man. He was the smallest man she'd ever seen. He was smaller than Teddy Fats, her special bear. Smaller even than anything. Her eyes got wider and wider still as she watched him tip-toe across the frozen grass. Then very, very slowly, she reached into her pocket.

The little man froze. He turned his gnomish face towards her, little eyes wide and startled. His surprise would have made her laugh except that she saw he was more scared-surprised than ha-ha-it's-a-joke-surprised. He had white hair, she saw, all curly like her own, and a little staff with feathers dangling from the top end.

"Don't go," she whispered.

The gnome trembled at the sound of her voice. He balanced on his toe-tips, ready to flee, but then Christine brought her hand out of her pocket and very slowly placed the thing she was holding in it onto the walk. It was the smallest little red wagon, which belonged with her playhouse set, and on it was a cookie. A chocolate chip cookie—which had to be better than acorns, she'd decided. Moving very slowly, she gave the wagon a push. It rolled towards the gnome who still looked like he was trying to make up his mind whether to stay or run.

The wagon came to a stop about a half foot from him. Christine could see his nostrils quivering as he smelled the cookie.

"It's for you,' she said. "My name's Christine. What's yours?"

The gnome moved closer to the wagon. He touched it with his tiny hand. His voice, when he replied, was very high pitched—the way a mouse's might sound, Christine thought, if a mouse could talk.

"Tomkin Furley," he piped. "That's my name and my name, too!"

Christine was delighted. "Do you like choco—"

The front door banged open behind her and Christine turned quickly to see her stupid big brother standing there.

"Holy jeez, Christine! What are you doing out here?" He had his ski jacket and touque on and was most likely going to his girlfriend's, Christine supposed, which didn't excuse him coming out here and ruining the best thing that had ever happened to her. She turned to look for Tomkin, but he was gone. Then she smiled. So was the wagon and cookie.

"Mum's going to kill you when she finds out," her brother informed her.

"Only if you tell her."

"Well, what *were* you doing out here?"

"Gnoming," she said with a little secret smile.

"You're nuts," he said as he brought her back inside, but he never did tell their parents.

When Christine woke up on Christmas morning, a week or so after that night, she took Teddy Fats from the pillow beside her and plonked him down on the table with all the rest of her toys. Two dolls, a stuffed bunny, a wooden soldier and a miniature rocking horse were all sitting around the small Christmas tree where she'd placed them last night. The tree was only a foot high and made of plastic, but it *looked* liked a Christmas tree and had tinsel and three ornaments on it, and it had some lights that really worked when you plugged them in, which Christine proceeded to do.

"Let's see what Santa brought you," she told them.

There were lots of little presents, all neatly wrapped, sitting under the tree. She knew what was in each one because she'd wrapped them yesterday afternoon. All by herself. She reached for the first one, a special one because it was the little scarf she'd knitted for Teddy Fats, but then she frowned and picked up another one instead. She frowned because she didn't know where it had come from and she picked it up because she wanted to see what was inside. It had a little tag on it that said "Christine" in the smallest of spidery little scripts. When she shook it, something rattled inside.

She opened it up and found a big yellow claw in it, with a little piece of paper to go with it. The paper, in the same spidery script, told her, after she'd puzzled all the words out very carefully:

> *This is the claw*
> *of the basement bogan*
>   *who also lived under your bed.*
> *I've banished him once*
> *and banished him twice,*
> *he'll never more bother you*
> *all through your life,*

you can sleep through the night,
snuggly and tight,
with never a worry instead.

And it was signed: "Tomkin Furley, which is my name."

Christine jumped to her feet and ran to the window to look down at the neighbour's hedge. And there she saw, or thought she saw, a little hand wave to her once and a flash of red that might have been a red wagon, and then they were gone and she never did see them again, though she looked very hard.

But she kept the claw under her pillow and she did sleep snuggly and tight, because she knew the thing in the basement was gone. And if Opa Jan was wrong sometimes, well he was right sometimes, too. And if she never did see Tomkin Furley again, the little things that she left for him by the hedge from time to time were never there the next day, and sometimes, even when she was older, she heard his little piping voice, singing to her on the wind, and it was always at that time just between the day and the night, when things are very magical anyway. ✑

Oakey Bedokey

IT WAS AUTUMN AND Jack o'Red was busy painting all the trees in the Tall Wood with many bright colours. After painting a leaf, the Wind would blow it dry—so dry that the leaf would sail from the tree with Jack o'Red chasing merrily after it. As the day wound on, and after all their painting and blowing and chasing, Jack and the Wind were both so tired that they had to plunk themselves down under a big tall oak tree to catch their breath.

"Look at that," Jack o'Red said, pointing to a wee tiny oak sapling.

The Wind pushed a tangle of feathery hair from her eyes and looked at the small tree. Standing with its brothers and sister, it was the littlest one of all.

"It's *so* small," she said.

Jack looked at the big paint brush in his hand and shook his head. From the bag at his side, he took a very tiny paint brush. The bells on the curled tips of his shoes jingled as he approached the little oak. He took the smallest of dabs of red paint, and an even tinier one of yellow, and one even smaller still of brown, and painted the few little leaves that the sapling had. When he was done, the Wind came and stood at his side and blew very softly on the leaves to dry them.

The sapling shook at the touch of her breath. One by one the wee leaves trembled and drifted to the ground. Without its autumn cloak, the little tree shivered, thin and small in the chilly air.

The Wind sighed.

"When winter comes it will be colder still," she said. "I'm afraid this one won't see the springtime— it's so small and weak."

Jack o'Red nodded sadly. He looked at the other saplings, growing tall and straight and strong.

"He won't last the winter," he agreed, looking at the drooping skinny branches of the smallest sapling.

"It needs a friend," the Wind said.

Suddenly she smiled and tugged at Jack's arm.

"Come, oh come," she said.

Off she went, swift as the…well, as swift as the Wind which she was. Jack o'Red hurried after her, his toe-bells ringing. He splattered the leaves of the trees as he ran by them—red and yellow and some colours in between. Over one hill and a second they went until they came to a small cabin that stood at the edge of the Tall Wood.

"Tap, tap," the Wind tapped on the windowpane.

Jack o'Red stood on his tiptoes to peer in and told his bells to be quiet. He saw a woman reading a book by the fire, which crackled merrily in an old iron wood stove. He saw a man washing the dishes.

"Tap, tap," the Wind tapped again.

Then Jack saw a little boy who looked up from his place by the fire to see the two faces peering in at him from the window.

"Come with us, little boy," the Wind whispered.

The little boy's name was Adam, but though the Wind knew many things, she didn't know that.

The woman looked up from her book and said to her husband, "My the wind is blustery today."

She glanced at the window, and so did her husband, but they were older than the little boy (after all, they were his parents), so they didn't see anything at all. But Adam put on his hat and his coat, then his scarf and his boots, then (just to be sure he'd be warm) some mittens, and asked his parents if he could go out to play.

When they said yes, he opened the door and the Wind laughed around him. Jack o'Red flung his paintbrush about in excitement and some paint splattered on Adam's coat, but the Wind blew very quick and hard (just for a moment) and the paint soon dried and flaked away.

"Come with us," she said.

"Where are we going?" Adam asked.

"Into the Tall Wood," Jack o'Red said.

Adam looked back at the cabin.

"I mustn't," he said. "I'm not allowed to go in there by myself."

"But you'll be with us," the Wind whispered and Jack o'Red's toe-bells jingled as he hopped about from one foot to the other.

"Do come, do come!" he cried.

Once more Adam said that he couldn't, and then that he shouldn't, but since he wouldn't actually be *alone*, in the end he nodded his head. So Jack o'Red took him by one hand, and the Wind took him by the other, and off they flew as quickly as…well, as quickly as the Wind at Adam's side. They followed the trail of paint that Jack had marked with his paint brush, deep and deeper still into the Tall Wood, until they came to where the little sapling stood shivering and small.

"Oh dear," the Wind said. "It's frozen already."

"Too late, too late," Jack o'Red said.

And indeed, to see the little tree, it seemed that way. But Adam ran up to it with a tear trickling down his cheek at the sad sight of it. He took off his scarf and wrapped it around the tiny trunk (which was so narrow about that even Adam could put his hand around it). Then he took off his mittens and stuck them on the ends of the two biggest branches (which weren't very big at all, really), and he leaned very close to the sapling and whispered comfortingly to it.

The other saplings watched Adam doing this and shook their boughs.

"A waste of time," they said. "That sapling will never be a tree. It's too small to be an oak. Too weak, too frail."

The big old oak tree watched Adam doing this and its bigger boughs shook sadly.

"Too late," it said. "Too small."

The Wind fluttered her windy fingers and Jack o'Red painted the whole of his sleeve a very sad blue.

But Adam didn't pay any attention to them at all. He hugged the tree and fixed the scarf so that it would warm as much of the little sapling as possible and pulled the mittens on tighter.

"Oh please," he said in a very small voice. "Don't die."

And then a wonderful thing happened.

The tiny sapling shivered again. But this time it began to grow smaller, as though it was pulling its little branches into itself. The two biggest branches (which still weren't very big at all) became arms, and Adam's mittens were on them. It pulled its roots up from the ground and they became legs. And then, all of a sudden (or perhaps it was even quicker than that), Adam was holding a little oak-boy in his arms who had a hat shaped like an acorn and oak leaves for a vest and Adam's scarf around his neck. He had big sad eyes that brightened when he looked at Adam.

"Oakey Bedokey!" Adam said. "That's who you are."

Oakey Bedokey smiled, for that was his name, though the Wind hadn't known that either.

The other saplings turned their backs.

"That's not a proper tree at all," they muttered.

The big oak tree turned its back as well.

"That boy never came from an acorn of mine!" it cried.

But Jack o'Red danced until his bells filled the whole wood with music, and the Wind blew this way and that until squirrels and rabbits (and even a raccoon who was up and about early that day) went hurrying home for umbrellas because they thought it was going to storm. And Adam took his new friend by the hand and they walked home together and, there in the cabin at the edge of the Tall Wood, they lived with Adam's mother and father and his little sister, forever and ever, and they were very happy indeed.

Sometimes in the Autumn, Jack o'Red would come and peer through the window at them. And often the Wind would come sneaking up on them and blow their hair into their eyes, then sail away laughing. And the other oak saplings grew into tall dour giants and never did know what they had missed by being what they were, rather than what their little brother had turned out to be. ❧

Maple Sugar

THIS IS A STORY I got from Jack o'Red and I know it's true, because while Jack plays tricks, he never tells lies.

Now every child knows that if you lose your way in the forest, the safest thing to do is stay in one spot until your parents find you. But once, when Kmoré was very young, she got lost in the woods near the cabin where she lived with her parents and her brother.

Because she lived so close to the forest, she wasn't frightened of the forest itself. But it was a little scary not knowing exactly where home was. And it was late in the afternoon, too. It would be getting dark soon and, though Kmoré wasn't exactly afraid of the dark either, being alone in both the forest and the dark was a little too much.

She tried walking in one direction for awhile, and then another, but neither was right and soon she was too tired to go any further. It was getting awfully dark under the trees. And there were an awful lot of them. They were terribly tall and beginning to look more like big dark giants than like trees.

The pines were the worst because they were the very biggest—enormous giant-like shapes in grim green cloaks, with pointy heads and huge branchy hands that all seemed to be reaching for her.

Creak.

Groan.

The sound of their arms as they moved, gnarly hands swooping down at her, snagging at her clothes and hair, was altogether too scary.

Crying a little—but only a little, for she was, after all, a brave sort of a little girl—she started to run. She was racing through the forest, faster and faster, when suddenly she broke free from the pine woods into a meadow dotted with maple trees and maple saplings.

Her heart was pounding as she stopped to look about herself. It was a little lighter here, out from under the pines, and even though the sky was darkening, she could make out the rich colours of the maple leaves.

Now she felt a little better. She liked maple trees, especially now in the autumn, when their leaves were turning all red and gold and yellow and orange. Kmoré liked leaves. She collected them and she'd probably have gone looking for a really good maple leaf to add to her collection, if it wasn't for the fact that she was still lost.

Very lost.

After awhile, being brave didn't help much. Leaning against a maple sapling, she listened to the wind murmur in its branches and began to cry in earnest.

The Wind wasn't really murmuring in the sapling's branches, though this was something Kmoré couldn't know. It takes very special eyes to be able to see into Faerie, and very special ears to hear what faeries are saying. So Kmoré couldn't see or hear what was happening in the tree just above her head. But I can tell you, for Jack o'Red was there and he saw it all.

Sitting just a few branches above Kmoré's head was the little spirit of the sapling against which Kmoré was leaning. She was sort of brownish, much like the young sapling's branches, and she had a jolly sweet look about her, which came, I suppose, from her maple syrup. (Have you ever tasted maple syrup? Isn't it sweet?) Her name was Maple Sugar. And she was talking to the wind.

"Oh, dear," she said. "I hate to hear anyone cry, but I especially hate to hear a brave little girl like that crying."

The Wind nodded. She was a faint presence in the air—like a gossamer spiderweb in the morning, sparkling with dew. Hard to see even with eyes that can see into Faerie.

"What shall we do to help her?" Maple Sugar asked.

It couldn't be something like taking the lost girl by the hand and leading her home because when trees spirits do that, they lose their own homes.

"I could blow her home," the Wind said.

"Oh, wouldn't that be nice? Blown helter-skelter through the forest, snagging on branches and banging your head on the ground. I don't think so."

"I'd blow her gently."

"I have a better idea," Maple Sugar said. And then she leaned close to the Wind and whispered in her ear.

"That's very clever," the Wind said.

Maple Sugar beamed at the praise. She was wearing a dress made of maple leaves. Plucking one leaf—the brightest, reddest one of all—she let it flutter to the ground before Kmoré's eyes.

For a long moment nothing happened. But then Kmoré reached for the leaf. Just before her fingers touched it, the Wind drifted down from her perch beside Maple Sugar and plucked it from the ground. She took it a step or two away—in the direction of Kmoré's home—then let it fall again.

Kmoré rubbed the tears from her eyes and got slowly to her feet. She stepped over to where the leaf lay and reached for it again. Again the Wind took it away. Kmoré thought she heard a giggle and turned sharply to see if it was maybe her brother laughing, but there was no one there. At least no one *she* could see. Maple Sugar pressed her knuckles against her mouth to stop herself from giggling again.

And so they went: Kmoré reaching for the leaf, the Wind blowing it out of her reach, and Maple Sugar following behind, giggling at the funny parade they made going through the darkened forest.

As it grew darker, the leaf began to glow a little so that Kmoré could still follow it, down into this hollow, up by this granite outcrop, through these trees. Soon they were very close to woods that Kmoré knew. And then she could see the twinkling yellow lights of the cabin where her parents would be worriedly waiting for her. They shone through the trees, warm and welcoming.

Kmoré gazed longingly at the glimmering leaf that lay so close, but so far.

"I think," she said aloud, "that someone has been helping me to get home." She turned a smiling face to the forest. "Oh, thank you, whoever you are."

"*I* think," Maple Sugar said to the Wind, "that I'd like to get to know this little girl better."

"If you go with her now," the wind said, "you'll lose your home in your tree."

Maple Sugar nodded. "That could be. But I'll gain something much better: a friend."

She ran out from the trees then and did whatever it is that faeries do when they want people to be able to see them. Kmoré gave a little cry of surprise at the maple spirit's sudden appearance, and then another cry, but of delight, at what a friendly sort of person this seemed to be. She picked Maple Sugar up and held her close—in Kmoré's arms the little maple spirit seemed to be just a doll.

And that's exactly what everyone else thought she was when Kmoré came in the cabin with her. But at nights in Kmoré's bed, and in the forest when they're alone, Maple Sugar becomes more than just a doll, and they talk and giggle and laugh and are the best of friends. 🕸

Tip & the Lion

IT WAS A BEDRAGGLED kitten that Tip found—tossed up from the ocean, it seemed, for she discovered it struggling weakly in the waves where the tide meets the sand. It was a tawny gold, the colour of a Serengeti lion: a tiny mewling creature, surely too young to have left its mother, but here it was all the same, shivering in Tip's arms, nuzzling at her T-shirt.

"Mom!" she called. "Look what I found!"

Christine came, expecting a shell, a piece of driftwood, a bit of sand-polished glass—any of the hundred and one treasures that her daughter could excitedly find on the stretch of beach in front of their house. Instead, she saw a small miracle in her daughter's arms.

"The poor thing," she said. "Let's get it home, Tip. It needs to be wrapped in a blanket and given some warm milk."

"It's too little to be swimming by itself, isn't it?"

"Much too little. Someone must have abandoned it."

Christine glanced over to the Pier further down the beach, shading her eyes in search of the culprit. For the kitten to have survived its swim, that was the closest place from which it could have been dropped. When she looked back at her daughter, Tip's face showed the struggle she was having with the last thing Christine had said.

"A-bam-mo-mit?"

Sometimes it was hard to remember that Tip was only five.

"It means someone didn't want it," Christine said.

"*I* want it, mom. We're going to keep it aren't we?"

Again Christine looked over toward the Pier. It was almost a quarter mile from where they stood, a long wooden arm reaching out into the sea. She could make out fishermen along its length, skateboarders on the ramp where it joined the parking lot. It was a very long swim. A real miracle.

"Of course we'll keep it," she said.

The kitten slept with Tip that night, after having been dried and fed and then shown off to her father Pete, who was marking papers out on the patio, and Granny Murray, who lived upstairs from them. Granny Murray owned the house and rented the downstairs to them, which was the only way they could have afforded to live here where the houses were snug, one against the other, all along the beachfront. She was Pete's grandmother and, next to her own parents, the best friend Tip had.

"Could be this isn't an ordinary kitten," Granny Murray said when she saw the bedraggled little thing, all fluffy now, amber eyes bright with interest for anything that moved. "Not a kitten born on the land."

"What do you mean?" Tip asked, her own eyes getting a little wide.

"Well," Granny Murray said, "there was a story I was told when I was young that the white caps of the waves are really the manes of the sea lions—not the kind that are like seals—"

Tip nodded sagely. Living in Seal Beach, with the

bronze seal statue at the end of the Pier, she knew exactly what her great grandmother meant.

"—but the kind that are like African lions, only they live in the ocean and they have white manes. Could be this kitten is one of their babies that got lost."

"Maybe," Tip said excitedly, "they're not supposed to go on land by themselves, like I'm not supposed to go in the water, but this one was bad and he did it anyway, and *that's* why he's lost."

"It could be."

"Should I put him back in the water?" Tip asked, wearing a solemn expression.

Granny Murray blinked, then quickly shook her head.

"Oh, don't be doing that," she said. "Maybe it's just a land kitty that you rescued from drowning—you wouldn't want to put him right back in a fix again, now would you?"

Tip cuddled the kitten with a considering look on her face that made Granny Murray smile.

"Was that a real story or just a pretend story?" Tip asked after a moment.

Granny Murray closed her eyes. She remembered growing up in this house and watching the lions playing in the waves when she was Tip's age. It hadn't mattered that they were just something that only she could see. Not to the little girl she'd been then. Nor to the old woman with a little girl's heart she was now.

"Sometimes," she said, "they can be the same thing."

Tip smiled, knowing exactly what her great grandmother meant, though it wasn't something that she could ever have put into words.

That night in her dreams, Tip saw the lions that live in the ocean. They came with a sound that Tip recognized as harping from one of her mother's tapes. They played in the waves—small animals the size of large dogs or seals—except for one, who was so big that if Tip leaned her head against him, her blonde hair mixing with his white mane, she would almost get lost in its thick tangles. He stepped out onto the beach and regarded her gravely, his eyes the same rich amber as those of her kitten, his fur the same tawny gold.

"Is it true?" Tip asked. "Did the kitten get lost?" When the lion nodded, she added, "Should I send him home?"

The lion shook his head.

"Don't you love him anymore?"

I love him better than I love life itself, the lion replied. His voice was a deep rumble in Tip's head.

"Then why can't he go home?"

Not that she wanted to lose the kitten. Already she loved it more than—well just about better than anything. Life itself was too complex a concept for her still. But she knew that if she were lost in the sea, she'd want to go home to her own family on the land just as soon as she could.

He must learn to be apart, the lion said.

That didn't make any sense to Tip at all. "A part of what?" she asked.

Of the wheel on which we turn. A part, and yet apart. His name is Marth.

Before Tip could ask what all of *that* meant, the lion turned and walked back into the ocean. When he dove beneath the waves, all the other lions followed suit. For a long moment Tip was alone on the beach, the night dark around her, the stars impossibly high above her. Then she turned in her bed, and walked into other dreams, but those she didn't remember in the morning.

During the summer days, the beach got crowded as soon as the sun burned the morning mists away and it stayed that way until the people went home for supper. When Tip's family could have the beach mostly to themselves was the time that Pete would put away his work—research for a book he was writing, now that the school year was done—and they'd go down to the water where he'd body surf while Tip and Christine walked along the shore.

Sometimes Christine would sit and watch her husband swim, thinking of the next chapter in the book she was writing. Then Tip would wander on by herself, but not far. She searched for treasures with Marth—just a lanky kitten still, but getting bigger every day—at her heels. When she'd finally return to her mother's side, Marth would lounge on the sand beside her and stare out at the waves with an intent expression. Then Tip would remember her dream and Granny Murray talking about real and pretend stories, saying, "Sometimes they can be the same thing."

She wondered if it was the same thing with dreams.

As the summer went by, Marth grew from a gangly teenager into a big tawny cat. He was interested in everything—not just the things that cats are normally interested in, like balls of wool or chasing a string tied to a stick, but everything. When the TV was on, he'd sit and watch just as intently as everyone else did. When Christine played her music, he seemed to listen with as much appreciation. When Pete was working, Marth would sit on his lap and look as though he was studying too. And just like Tip, he loved to go upstairs and listen to Granny Murray tell stories.

Tip's birthday was on Halloween and as the days drew closer to it, the ocean colder, the beach more desolate, she'd sometimes find Marth missing for hours at a time, only to spy him coming back from across the beach, his paws salty wet, an odd look in his amber eyes. And then Tip would remember her dream even more strongly. She'd see that lion again and the memory of his voice would ring in her head.

A part and yet apart of the wheel on which we turn.

She still wasn't exactly sure what it meant, even though she was going on six now, but thought it might be something like what Granny Murray said about real and pretend sometimes being the same. She'd imagine a tall Ferris Wheel rising out of the tide, in every swinging gondola a pair of lions, the salty water dripping from their tawny fur, their amber eyes gleaming in the starlight.

And then her imagination would begin to work as though someone else was using it to tell her a story, instead of it just being her pretending to herself. She'd see the big lion in a gondola all to himself. Round and round it would go, under the waves, high up to the stars, back under again. And then one time it would come out of the waves and it would be empty. When that happened, Tip would hug Marth to her chest and a tear, salty as the tide that had swallowed the lion, would form in each of her eyes.

Lying in her bed the night before her birthday, Tip heard that sound again—the harping that played against the rise and fall of the waves as the tide pushed them back and forth against the shore. The house was quiet, except for that sound. Her parents were asleep— just like she should be. She lay still, trying to be good, but when Marth came and licked her cheek, then jumped down from the bed and padded out of the bedroom, she couldn't do anything but follow.

It was being very bad, and she knew it, but she couldn't help herself. It was like being in a dream, and maybe she was only dreaming, still lying in her bed, only imagining that she was following Marth out onto the patio and then across the sand to where the tide met the land and the sea lions were waiting. A time when real and pretend were the same.

The sea lions weren't playing tonight. The starlight shone on their tawny flanks as they crouched in a circle around the big lion who was lying on the sand, a weary look in his old amber eyes. Tip saw the Ferris Wheel of her imagination go up, come down, the big lion's gondola empty as it rose from the waves.

Marth approached the lion and lay down on the sand, nose to nose with him, and a very strange thing began to happen. As the harping rose and fell to the tempo of the waves, the big lion grew smaller, and Marth grew larger. When Marth was the same size as the old lion had been, there was only a shadow lying on the sand in front of him—a small dark shape that leaked away into the sand until all that remained was a small amber stone.

Marth was the big lion now. He turned and approached Tip, the rasp of his tongue rough against her cheek, then he led the sea lions back into the waves. The starlight caught their glimmering shapes as they swam out towards the horizon, before the waters closed over them and they were gone.

Tip blinked away tears, but they wouldn't stop coming. She went down on her knees and stared out across the water. Slowly she picked up the stone. When she touched it, the stone grew warm in her palm and the old lion's voice spoke in her head.

It was his time on the wheel, for my time was done. He was apart from us, gaining knowledge, and now he is a part of us again.

"I...I don't want him to be gone," Tip said. "I don't want any of you to be gone."

You gave him the greatest gift of all, dearheart—an understanding of love. Marth means wonder in our old language, and wonder he had in plenty, but he needed to be wise, too. And he needed to know how to love. One day you will understand, that because of that gift, we will never be gone.

The stone grew cool in Tip's hand and though she called out to the lion, and to Marth, the stone neither warmed nor spoke again. Instead a hand touched her shoulder and she looked up to find Granny Murray standing beside her. There was a look of sorrow in her great-grandmother's eyes, but a look of joy, too.

"I had a sea kitten once," she said, "and I had to give it up, too."

"Did...didn't it make you sad, Granny?"

"Very sad. But happy, too. When you're touched by magic, nothing's ever quite the same again. What really makes me sad is all those people who never have the chance to know that touch. They're too busy, or they just don't hold with make-believe, so they shut the door without really knowing it was there to be opened in the first place."

"Like real and pretend sometimes being the same?"

Granny Murray nodded. "But mostly knowing that the wonder's always there. You might not get to see it, you might just catch a glimpse, but it's always there. Knowing that is it's own kind of magic."

"I'm still going to miss him."

"I know, dear."

For a long time they watched the waves roll in and out, catching glimpses of shapes playing in the whitecaps, or perhaps just thinking they did, which was almost the same thing. Then hand in hand they walked back home across the beach. ❧